"To Zander Dane"—J.E.

"To my cats, rats, and pet rocks!"—A.B.

STERLING CHILDREN'S BOOKS
New York

An Imprint of Sterling Publishing Co., Inc.
1166 Avenue of the Americas
New York, NY 10036

STERLING CHILDREN'S BOOKS
and the distinctive Sterling Children's Books logo are
registered trademarks of Sterling Publishing Co., Inc.

ISBN 978-1-4549-2172-1

Distributed in Canada by Sterling Publishing Co., Inc.
c/o Canadian Manda Group, 664 Annette Street
Toronto, Ontario, Canada M6S 2C8
Distributed in the United Kingdom by GMC Distribution Services
Castle Place, 166 High Street, Lewes, East Sussex, England BN7 1XU
Distributed in Australia by NewSouth Books
45 Beach Street, Coogee, NSW 2034, Australia

For information about custom editions, special sales,
and premium and corporate purchases, please contact Sterling Special Sales
at 800-805-5489 or specialsales@sterlingpublishing.com.

Manufactured in China

Lot #:
1 2 3 4 5 6 7 8 9 10
08/17

sterlingpublishing.com

Design by Irene Vandervoort

FRANKENBUNNY

by Jill Esbaum
illustrated by Alice Brereton

STERLING CHILDREN'S BOOKS
New York

You know monsters aren't real, right?

Yeah. Me, too.
Except for this one time
when my big brothers
made me forget.

Don't think that could happen to you? HA!
Pretend you're me.

There you are, fixing your bike,
minding your own beeswax,
when suddenly—

"Hey, Spencer," says Leonard.
"We have to tell you something."

"Yeah," says Bertram.
"It's about monsters.
Be brave, little brother."

"I am brave,"
you say.

Brave is easy in
the sunshine.

"All monsters are dangerous," says Leonard.
"But Frankenbunny's the worst!"

"No such thing as monsters," you say.

Your brothers leave.

Whew! Because thinking about monsters makes your whiskers twitch.

"If I were you," says Leonard, "I wouldn't play in here."

"Yeah," says Bertram. "Frankenbunny loves dark places."

You know you shouldn't ask, but . . .

"What does he look like?"

"Imagine crusty fangs,"
says Leonard. "And ginormous
paws that could smash you flat."
You imagine.
"I'd hide."

Bertram goes, "*Pfft.* Frankenbunny has flashing red eyes. Those babies can see through *anything*."

Instant goose bumps. "No way."

"Way."

Your heart starts to race. So do your feet.

"Ignore them, dear,"
says Mama.

Doesn't help.

"FLASHING RED EYES!"

"Mama-a-a-a!"

"Mama's at her book club," says Papa. "What's the trouble, Spence?"

"Monsters," you report. "Leonard and Bertram say Frankenbunny's the worst."

Papa flips a veggie burger. "You know monsters aren't real, right?"

And just like that, the scared leaks out of you.

“Right,” you say. “Not real. Everybody knows that, heh, heh.”

“Attaboy.”

Brave is easy around Papa.

But at bedtime, Leonard makes his voice low and spooky.

"They say he hides in closets."

"Yeah," says Bertram. "He bursts out at midnight, and—*chomp!*—you're a goner."

You peek at the closet.
It's big enough. A monster
could be hiding in there.
Still . . .

"Papa says there's no such
thing as m-m-monsters,"
you whisper.

"Oh, they're real, all right,"
says Leonard.
"Papa just doesn't want
you to worry."

You worry.

Brave is *hard* in the dark!

The next morning, you wake up to good old sunshine—and news that makes you dance: Your brothers have gone to play at a friend's.

You aren't even thinking about Frankenbunny as you go to get a coat. But then—

Wait . . . what's that?

One look at the monster your brothers drew, with its
CRUSTY FANGS!
GINORMOUS PAWS!
FLASHING RED EYES!
and you know what you're holding:
A plan. A dirty, rotten plan.
OPERATION SCARE SPENCER!!!
•Oven mitts
•Lights
•Fireworks?
•Dark clothes
•BIG GLOVES!
•Paper
•Glue
•Plants
•Football helmet
•Ballooooons
•Snacks!!!
I AM FRANKENBUNNY!
AHHH!

Prickles of *mad* burn your ears. **“ARRRGGGHHHH!”**

Those rats! you think. And you wish *they* could know how it feels to be scared.

Whisker-twitchy scared.

Goose-bumpy scared. *Cry-and-run-to-Mama* scared.

OPERATION SCARE SPENCER!!!
I AM
FRANKENBUNNY
Football helmet

That night, you wait a long time for the rats to run out of Frankenbunny talk.

When they're finally asleep . . .

. . . you sneak out of bed . . .

. . . and tiptoe to the closet.

"I AM FRANKENBUNNY!"

"RUN!"
#1

"RUN FOR YOUR LIVES!"

After all the screaming and blubbering,

after Papa's "Nothing in the closet, see?"

after Mama's "Back to bed, everybunny . . ."

You start to feel sorry.

Your brothers have been rats, yes.

But, well . . .

"Hey, guys? Um, listen. I have to tell you something. It's about Frankenbunny."

LA LA LA LA LA LA LA"

You understand. Brave is hard in the dark.

Not for you, though.
Not anymore.
You know monsters aren't real. *You* know there's no such thing as Frankenbunny.

You'll make sure your big brothers know it, too.

First thing in the morning.

PROBABLY.

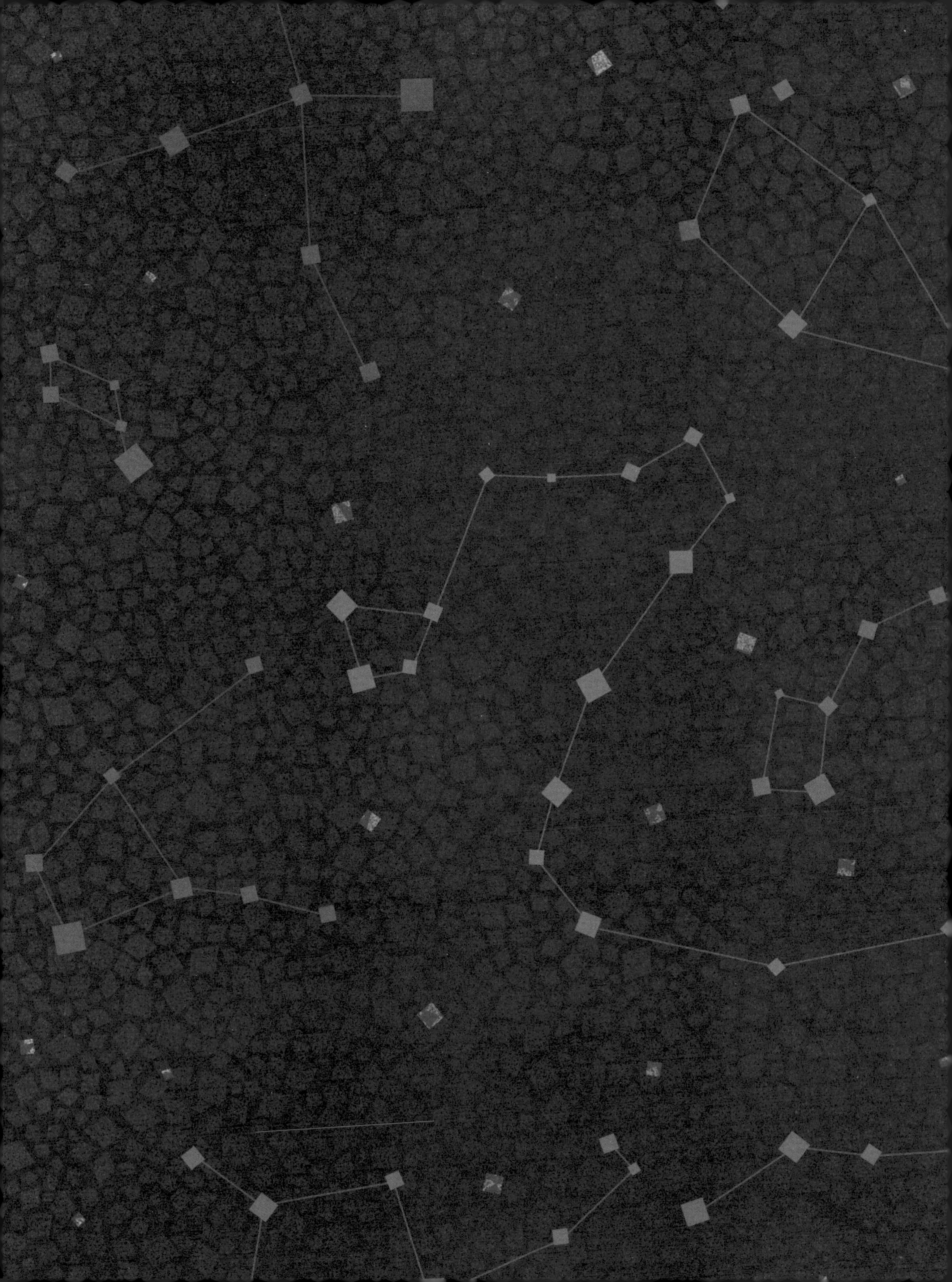